Library of Congress Cataloging-in-Publication Data

Yeoman, John.
Old Mother Hubbard's dog dresses up / John Yeoman and
Quentin Blake.—1st American ed.
p. cm.
Summary: When Old Mother Hubbard complains to her dog about
the ragged condition of his coat, he resorts to wearing a variety of
disguises and drives her to distraction.
ISBN 0-395-53358-9
[1. Dogs—Fiction. 2. Stories in rhyme.] I. Blake, Quentin.
II. Title.
PZ8.3.Y460h   1990   89-27026
[E]—dc20   CIP
                                                        AC

Text copyright © 1989 by John Yeoman
Illustrations copyright © 1989 by Quentin Blake
First American edition 1990
Originally published in Great Britain in 1989
by Walker Books Ltd.

Printed in Italy
10 9 8 7 6 5 4 3 2 1

Old Mother Hubbard's Dog

Dresses Up

John Yeoman & Quentin Blake

Houghton Mifflin Company
Boston 1990

Said Old Mother Hubbard, one dark winter's night,
While giving a bath to her goat,
"That dog looks as though he's been having a fight:
I wish he'd take pride in his coat."

The very next morning she had a great shock
Which made her feel weak at the knees,
For there was the dog, wearing beret and smock,
Painting pictures of birds in the trees.

He went indoors, leaving his paintings to dry;

She followed – and what do you think?

He was dressed as a sailor, a patch on one eye,

With a small fleet of boats in the sink.

Said Old Mother Hubbard, "You're getting me down;
Oh, won't you behave yourself, please?"
But five minutes later, got up like a clown,
He was juggling with pieces of cheese.

So Old Mother Hubbard lay down to relax:
She felt a slight ache in the head.
But dressed as a burglar, with crowbar and axe,
The dog stole the legs off the bed.

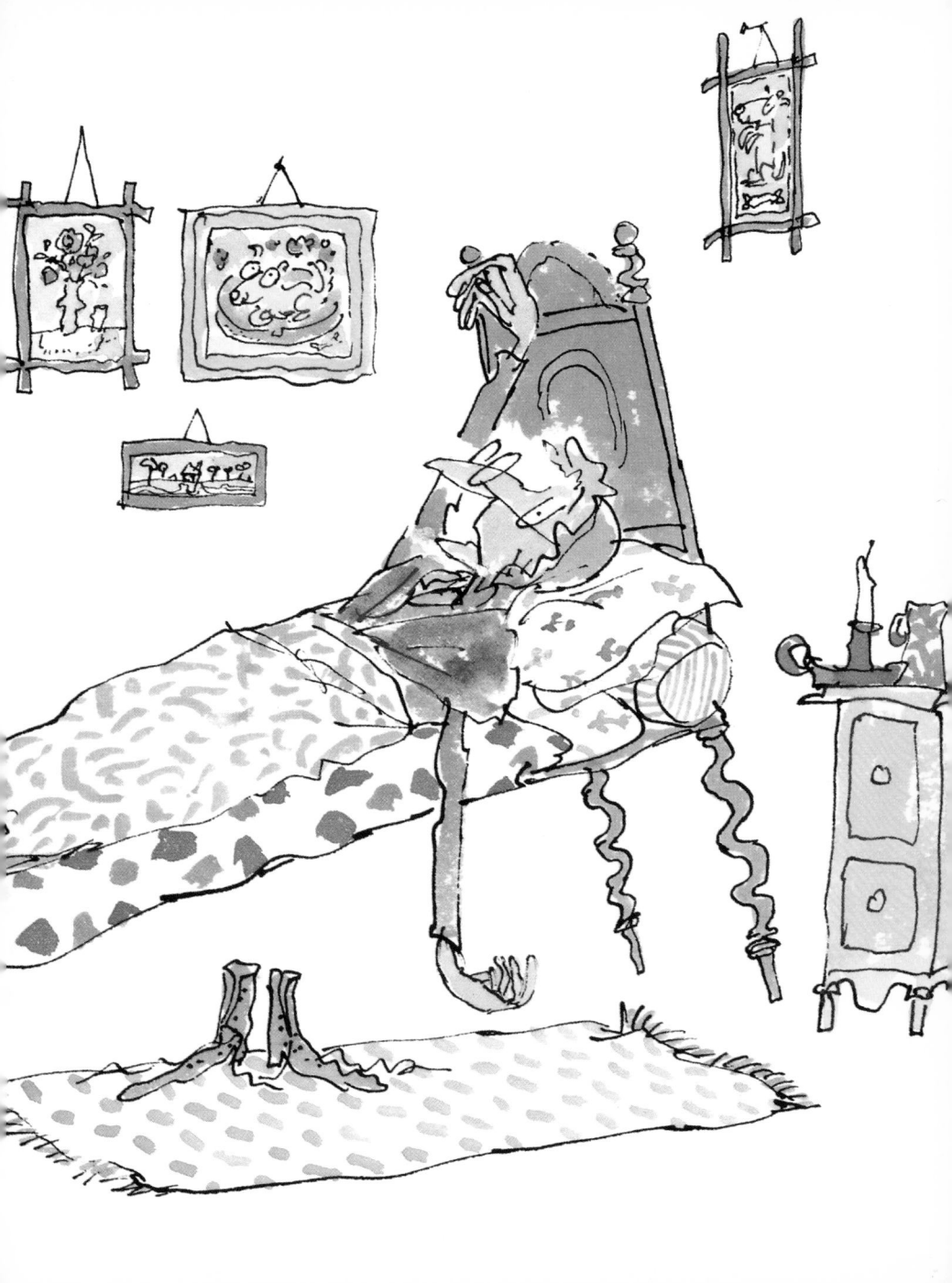

Then Old Mother Hubbard heard no noise at all.
Now, did that mean mischief or not?
She found him downstairs, dressed in bonnet and shawl,
And gurgling away in his cot.

"Oh, do something useful!" the poor woman cried.

The dog scratched his head, thinking hard.

Then, in helmet and armor, he clattered outside,

Giving chase to the mice in the yard.

Thought Old Mother Hubbard, while bolting the door,
"He's so disobedient and rude!
But I won't pass remarks on his coat any more:
He's better behaved in the nude."